BILLY AND THE MINI MONSTERS

Monsters go Green

ZANNA DAVIDSON

Illustrated by MELANIE WILLIAMSON

Meet Billy...

Billy was just an ordinary boy living an ordinary life, until **ONE NIGHT** he found five **MINI MONSTERS** in his sock drawer.

Gloop

Peep

Fang-Face

Captain Snott

Trumpet

Then he saved their lives, and they swore never to leave him.

We give you the Secret-Hairy-Snot-Tooth Oath of Devotion.

When he moved, Billy found ANOTHER monster.

Hello. My name's Sparkle-Boogey.

One thing was certain – Billy's life would never be the same **AGAIN**...

Contents

Chapter 1
Saving the Planet

It was Sunday night and Billy was at home with his Mini Monsters. They were all doing their favorite Sunday night things...

Fang-Face was secretly eating Billy's socks.

Sparkle-Boogey and Trumpet were playing "hunt the cheese."

Captain Snott was practicing superhero poses in front of the mirror...

I look so **HANDSOME!**

...and Peep was catching up on his reading.

"Billy, what are you reading?" asked Sparkle-Boogey.

"It's a book about **saving the planet**," said Billy.

We're learning about it at school.

"But why does the planet need saving?" asked Captain Snott.

"The planet's in trouble because of things *people* are doing," said Billy.

9

"Let's all look at my book."

WHAT'S HAPPENING TO OUR PLANET?

Planet Earth needs our help! The way we live is producing lots of pollution which is harming the planet. Sea levels are rising and many animals are losing their homes.

Forests are being chopped down to make space for cattle, crops and new homes.

The fuels we use to heat our homes, and drive vehicles, produce gases that trap in heat, so our planet gets warmer.

Planes are big polluters too.

As the planet warms, ice in the Arctic is melting. This makes life hard for lots of animals.

Pollution in rivers is a threat to fish and other creatures that live there.

Landfills are made up of rotting garbage that produces another planet-warming gas.

Plastic is ending up in the oceans, which harms wildlife.

"Oh no!" cried Peep. "We don't want animals to lose their homes." "Or for the planet to be full of garbage!" added Captain Snott.

Cows' burps and toots contain methane, another gas that causes global warming.

Dry places are getting drier.

Wet places are getting wetter.

Toots can change the Earth's climate!

It says toots are heating up the planet too!

"That's why we're having a

GO GREEN

week at school," said Billy.
"There's a **competition** too."

The student who
does the most to
help the environment
wins a prize.

"I want to do everything I can to
help the planet," Billy went on.
"So do we!" said Sparkle-Boogey.
"In that case," said Billy. "It's
time to **GO GREEN**!"

13

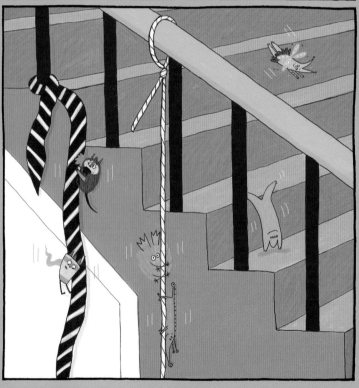

14

Chapter 2
Shoe Surprise

The next morning, Billy came down for breakfast feeling very excited.

Today, I'm going to help save the planet!

"First," said Billy's mom, "you need to explain these shoes."

"How did you get them so *green*?" asked his dad.

Suddenly, Billy knew **exactly** what had happened.

"I... um... had an accident," said Billy. "With a can of paint."

Billy's mom gave a small sigh. "I'll get the paint off while you get dressed," she said.

Back in his bedroom, Billy pulled open his sock drawer.

Did you like your shoe surprise?

Wasn't it a great idea!

Should we do your shirt next?

"Going green doesn't mean being *the color* green," Billy explained.

Oh!

"It's about doing good things for the planet," Billy went on.

THINGS YOU CAN DO AT HOME AND AT SCHOOL

Use as little plastic as possible

Recycle

Eat less meat and animal produce, like milk and cheese

Turn off the lights

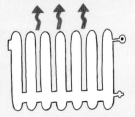

Turn down the heat and put on a sweater

Try not to waste water

"Look! The school gave us a chart of things we can try to do."

THINGS YOU CAN DO IN THE GARDEN AND OUTSIDE

Pick up litter

Walk or cycle to school if you can, rather than go by car

Make a bug hotel

Carry your own water bottle so you don't buy plastic bottles

Grow wild flowers

Create a hedgehog home

"Our school project this week is to do as many **green things** as we can. Then, on Friday, we tell everyone what we've done and they'll choose the winner."

"And today," said Billy, "we've got a school trip to the recycling center, to learn why recycling is good for the planet."

"Can we come too?" asked Fang-Face. "We're really sorry about your shoes."

We promise to be good.

We won't be any trouble.

"No way," said Billy. "The recycling center is full of **DANGEROUS MACHINES**. I'll tell you all about it when I'm back..."

As Billy was brushing his teeth...

I love school trips.

Me too.

Let's go to the recycling center.

We'll just stay inside Billy's bag and peek out.

Billy will never know!

Inside Billy's bag...

I've worked out how I'm going to save the planet!

How?

I'm going to stop eating Billy's clothes and start eating **TRASH**!

Then there'll be less litter. I'm a **GENIUS**!

29

Chapter 3
The Recycling Center

When they got inside, Billy's class stood for a moment, gazing at the huge machines.

"Welcome, everyone," said Miss Khan. "I'm the manager here. I'll explain how all these machines work, and there's a quiz for you to answer as well."

You can do the quiz with a friend.

"Will you do the quiz with me?" asked Billy's best friend, Ash. Billy nodded. "Definitely!"

"It all begins here," said Miss Khan, pointing to her right. "This grabber drops off the trash, and it falls onto the conveyor belt."

Isn't it great!

But Billy wasn't listening. He thought he'd seen something purple and furry moving along the conveyor belt...

"Billy! Are you paying attention?" asked Mr. Gritton, the teacher.

"Yes," said Billy, clearly not paying any attention at all.

"Wow!" said Ash.
"Did you hear that, Billy?"
Billy was rubbing his eyes. He
was sure he'd seen something blue
and slimy, coming out the
other end of the machine.

Am I imagining things?

"Billy," said Ash, "we've got to listen to Miss Khan, or we'll never be able to do the quiz."

But Billy was **too distracted**.

"I REALLY hope my Mini Monsters aren't here!" he thought. "They're supposed to be **SAFE AT HOME!**"

Billy!

But before Billy could get a good look around, Miss Khan showed everyone into a little cabin...

36

....and Billy had

NO CHOICE

but to follow.

Chapter 4
Gloop goes Missing

Miss Khan and the class huddled together inside the cabin.

"These workers are looking for items which can't be recycled," said Miss Khan, "like paint and plastic film, that might clog up the machine. Who can spot something?"

There's some paint in that can.

You're right!

What's that?

HAZARDOUS WASTE

He started waving, trying to get their attention.

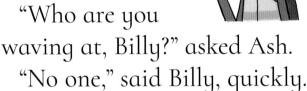

"Who are you waving at, Billy?" asked Ash.

"No one," said Billy, quickly.

I'm sure you waved!

I didn't wave.

Billy could tell he'd upset Ash and he really wanted to make things better, but his monsters were in **DANGER** – he had to get them back.

Thinking fast, Billy reached into his bag, pulled out his pencil case... and dropped it onto the conveyor belt.

Oh no! My pencil case.

While everyone was distracted, Billy bent down and whispered to the Mini Monsters.

Jump! NOW!

Five Mini Monsters jumped, just in time. But it was too late for Gloop. He was already heading **OUT OF THE CABIN**...

"Where does the conveyor belt go next?" asked Billy, panicking.

"Well!" said Miss Khan, eagerly, "Next up is a machine full of **GIANT SCREWS** to filter out the cardboard, followed by some rollers."

"And then," she went on enthusiastically, "there's a magnet to pick out scraps of metal. And last but not least, a **GIANT** SPINNING DRUM!"

"And after that?" asked Billy, in a small voice.

"The recyclable trash is squashed into bales," said Miss Khan. "And the rest is burned. Isn't that efficient! So amazing!"

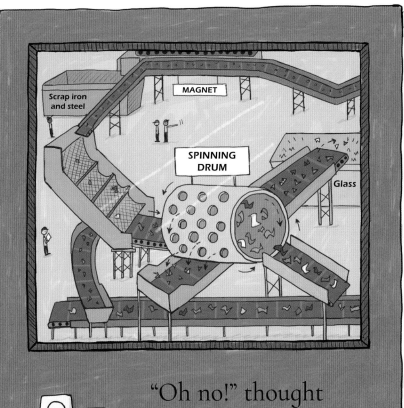

"Oh no!" thought Billy. "Gloop! I must save Gloop!"

Whew! That was hairy!

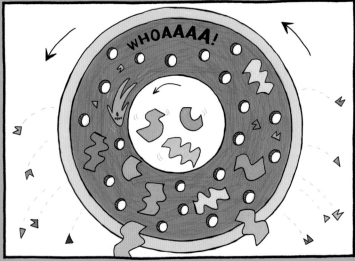

52

Chapter 5
Ash to the Rescue

Billy slipped out of the cabin. "Stay safe in my bag," he whispered to the Mini Monsters. "This place is **DANGEROUS** for small monsters."

Then he turned to see Ash standing behind him.

"Oh!" said Billy. "I, um, didn't see you there..."

"I thought we were supposed to be friends," said Ash. "*Best* friends."

We are best friends! I promise!

Then why are you ignoring me?

"I've got... a little... **problem**," said Billy, trying to explain.

"Can you tell me what it is?" asked Ash. "Maybe I can help?"

Billy *wished* he could tell Ash about the Mini Monsters...

It's supposed to be a secret.

It's fine. You don't have to tell me.

"Wait!" said Billy. "I'd still really like your help!"

Ash nodded. "Go on," he said.

"I've **lost something**," said Billy. "It's a sort of... toy. It's blue and gloopy with four eyes. And this might sound odd, but it's really **special** to me."

Billy and Ash searched up and
down the conveyor belts.

They looked
under the
conveyor belts...

Gloop?

...*behind* the
conveyor belts...

...but there was
NO SIGN
of Gloop.

"This place is **MASSIVE!**" thought Billy. "Gloop could be *anywhere*. We'll never find him." Just then, Billy's class came out of the cabin. Billy and Ash shuffled back into the line. Mr. Gritton looked at them, suspiciously.

"Finally," Miss Khan was saying, "this is where the baler machine squashes all the recycling into giant bales."

Maybe **Gloop's** in one of these? I'll never find him now...

"And that's the end of the tour," said Miss Khan.

"Thank you," said Mr. Gritton. "That was fascinating. Students, you can hand in the quiz on Friday."

Billy and Ash turned to go. Billy was trying very hard not to cry.

Billy! Quick! Over here.

"Is **this** what you're looking for?" asked Ash.

Billy bent down and gently picked up the very squished-looking blue thing.

"Yes, it is," he said, quietly. "Thank you, Ash."

Back on the bus, Billy bent down and whispered to Gloop.

Gloop? Gloop? Are you okay?

Gloop lay very still in his hand. Billy held his breath...

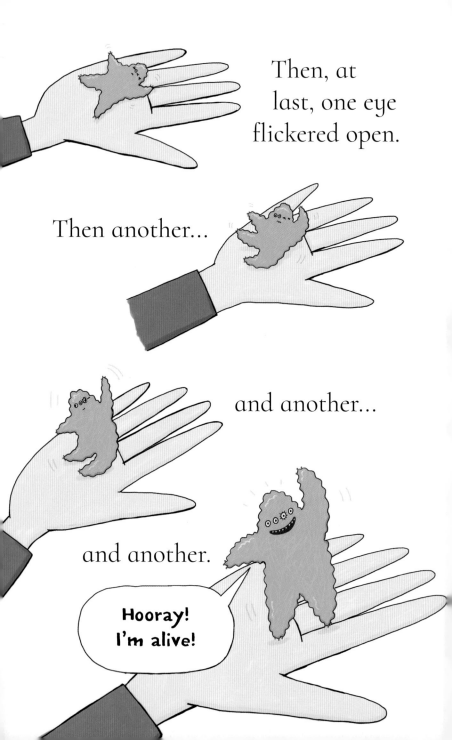

"You look a little... different," said Billy. "Do you feel okay?"

"I feel **GREAT**!" said Gloop. "Better than ever."

"Then that's what matters," said Billy, grinning.

Back at Billy's house...

We messed up Billy's school trip.

I know.

Let's make it up to him.

How?

We can help him win the **GO GREEN** competition!

65

66

Chapter 6
Green Heroes

On Friday morning, the Mini Monsters woke early.

"WOW!" said Billy.
"This is **amazing!**"

"What about you, Billy?" asked Peep. "What have you done for the competition?"

"I've written a **Going Green** song!" said Billy.

Billy's Going Green Song!

Be fantastic
Say no to plastic!
Look after bees
Plant lots of trees
Let's make a vow –
to save our
super planet
NOW!

As soon as Billy got to school, he laid everything out on the display table.

"That looks great, Billy," said Ash. "You're sure to win the competition."

Billy shook his head. "I couldn't do the Recycling Quiz. I know you'll say I can use your answers, but I didn't help you at all. And I don't mind if I don't win. The best thing was that you helped me find my toy."

"Do you want to come over to my house tomorrow?" Billy asked. "Definitely," said Ash.

Mr. Gritton came to Billy and Ash's table last of all.

"**Very impressive**," he said at last. "I think we have two winners here! Ash has won the Recycling Quiz and Billy has won Best Display."

Congratulations!

When he got home, Billy ran up to his bedroom, to show the Mini Monsters his prize.

"This isn't just for me," he said. "It's for all of us."

"I've got one more favor to ask," Billy went on. "Do you think I could tell Ash about you?"

"I think it's time," said Peep.

That night, Billy went to bed with a **big smile** on his face. "I learned how to help save the planet *and* Ash is going to meet the Mini Monsters. We're going to have so much **fun** together."

But then he heard a little sniff, coming from the sock drawer.

What's the matter, **Gloop**?

I didn't help you save the planet.

"Of course you helped," said Billy. "You're the greenest of us all. After all, you've been **recycled!**"

"So I have!" grinned Gloop.

Billy went back to bed. But he felt as if something was missing...

Suddenly, he knew *exactly*
what it was. "Trumpet!
There's **NO SMELL**!"
"I know!" said Trumpet.
"I've stopped eating cheese."

"Hooray for **GOING GREEN**!" said
Captain Snott. "Good night, Billy."
"Good night, my Mini
Monsters," said Billy.

77

All about the MINI MONSTERS

CAPTAIN SNOTT →

LIKES EATING: boogeys.

SPECIAL SKILL:
can glow in the dark.

SCARE
FACTOR:
5/10

← GLOOP

LIKES EATING: cake.

SPECIAL SKILL:
very stre-e-e-e-tchy.
Gloop can also swallow his own
eyeballs and make them reappear
on any part of his body.

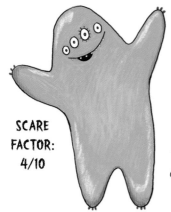

SCARE
FACTOR:
4/10

FANG-FACE →

LIKES EATING:
socks, school ties, paper, or
anything that comes his way.

SPECIAL SKILL:
has massive fangs.

SCARE
FACTOR:
9/10

TRUMPET →

LIKES EATING:
vegan cheese.

SPECIAL SKILL:
amazingly powerful
cheese-powered toots.

SCARE FACTOR:
7/10
(taking into
account his toots)

PEEP

LIKES EATING: very small flies.

SPECIAL SKILL: can fly (but
not very far, or very well).

SCARE FACTOR:
0/10 (unless you're afraid of
small hairy things)

SPARKLE-BOOGEY

LIKES EATING:
eco-glitter and boogeys.

SPECIAL SKILL:
can shoot out clouds
of glitter.

SCARE FACTOR:
5/10 (if you're scared of
pink sparkly glitter)

Series editor: Becky Walker
Designed by Brenda Cole
Cover design by Hannah Cobley
American editor: Carrie Armstrong

First published in 2021 by Usborne Publishing Ltd., Usborne House,
83-85 Saffron Hill, London EC1N 8RT, England. usborne.com © 2021,
2020 Usborne Publishing Ltd. The name Usborne and the Balloon
logo are Trade Marks of Usborne Publishing Ltd. All rights reserved.
No part of this publication may be reproduced, stored in a retrieval
system or transmitted in any form or by any means without the prior
permission of the publisher. AE. This edition first published in America
2021. EDC, Tulsa, Oklahoma 74146 usbornebooksandmore.com
Library of Congress Control Number: 2021935911